EDWURD FUDWUPPER
FIBBED BIG

Explained by FANNIE FUDWUPPER

With
BERKELEY BREATHED
Helping Slightly

A Storyopolis Book

 Little, Brown and Company
Boston New York London

Also by Berkeley Breathed

Goodnight Opus

The Last Basselope

Red Ranger Came Calling

A Wish for Wings That Work

Visit the artistry and humor of Berkeley Breathed at www.BerkeleyBreathed.com.

The author wishes to thank President Bill Clinton, without whose daily inspiration this particular story just plain wouldn't have come to mind.

A Storyopolis Book

Since its inception in 1995, Storyopolis, a multifaceted entertainment company, has been dedicated to celebrating and preserving the visual, oral, and written tradition of stories in all forms of media and to providing children and adults with the resources to "feed the mind and soul" through its unique art gallery and bookstore featuring the finest in creation in books and art.

www.storyopolis.com

First Edition

Library of Congress Cataloging-in-Publication Data
Breathed, Berke.
    Edwurd Fudwupper fibbed big / explained by Fannie Fudwupper ;
with Berkeley Breathed helping slightly.—1st ed.
        p.   cm.
    Summary: Edwurd's little sister comes to the rescue when Edwurd's humongous fib
lands him in trouble with a three-eyed alien from another galaxy.
    ISBN 0-316-10675-5
    [1. Honesty—Fiction. 2. Sisters and brothers—Fiction. 3. Stories in rhyme.]   I. Title.
PZ8.3.B7394 Ed 2000
[E]—dc21   99-043717

10 9 8 7 6 5 4 3 2 1

MON-SP

Printed in Spain
D.L. TO: 186-2000

The illustrations for this book were done in watercolor and acrylic on illustration board.
The text type was set in Leawood Book, and the display type is Decotura.

For Allyson—.

From a long line of liars, there's none higher upper...

Than my fibbing big brother,

The Edwurd Fudwupper.

There he is now,
I know *just* what he's doing:
He's thinking of who could be next for some fooling.
Edwurd's been cooking up fibs full of phooey;
He'll serve them up SWEET, all gooey with hooey.

Last week he fibbed big and told Mabel Dill,
"I read you've been voted the queen of Brazil!
They want you to come!
Bikinis! BRING TEN!"
I think Mabel went; no one's seen her since then.

Yes, he thought them up long
And he thought them up tall,
But did he think much of *me?*

No, not much.
Not at all.

Like the time he fibbed big
And told Ben and Dinky
That I had been borne by
A poodle named Stinky.

That wasn't so nice,
But that fib I'd forgive...
If only he liked me,
Or noticed I live.

Early this morning he did it again.
He whacked a baseball and things smashed in the den.

Dad rushed on over and found Mom's cracked pig,
Then Edwurd Fudwupper fibbed way WAY TOO BIG.

"It's all truly, clearly, quite
simple, you know.
The whole thing was done
by two pigs from Plu-to."

"They were cruising by Earth,
Looking down from above...
When they spotted Mom's pig
And fell deeply in love."

"So they dropped one pig here,
He just could not resist—

That passionate porker
Insisted a kiss!"

"But he leaned in too far
And Mom's pig hit the ground.

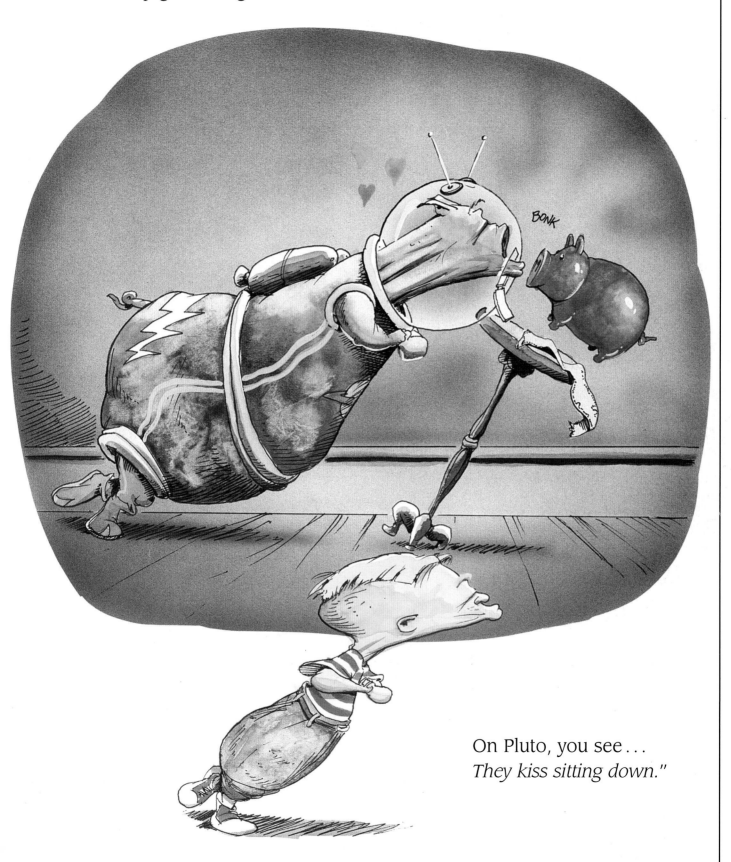

On Pluto, you see . . .
They kiss sitting down."

"Then he left brokenhearted, upset and unseen,
And his ship picked him up with a pig-lifting beam."

"And that's all, that's the truth,"
Said Ed the Fib Slinger.

In the whole of fib history,
A WHOPPING humdinger.

Then a yelp! And a howl! And a scream from nearby!
Lorna-Mae Loon had been listening outside.
"Mabel Dill," she cried loudly,
"has been missing for days! . . .

. . . SHE MUST'VE BEEN GRABBED BY THOSE PIG-LIFTING RAYS!"

MISSING

She got to a phone and screamed loud 'n' shrill:
"Space monster piggies have nabbed Mabel Dill!
They're coming for me!
And they're coming for you! . . .

And that's *just* what they did! They came for space pigs!
With planes and with tanks and with loud whirligigs!
Oh, it was dreadful! A real world stopper!
All from an Edwurd Fudwupper fat whopper!

They pointed their loudspeaker dishes to space
And those generals roared till red in the face:
"Now listen out there! We'll shoot! Yes, we will!
Come back here at once—

Edwurd watched all of this for quite a long time,
But people were staring at something behind.
Oh rats, Edwurd thought. How much more could there be?...

A face filled the sky
        from the hills to the sea!
It did not look happy,
        nor pleasant, nor soft;
In fact that big thing
        looked somewhat TICKED OFF!
It was purple and green
        with an eye on its snoot.
It opened its mouth, roaring,
        "Who started this hoot?"

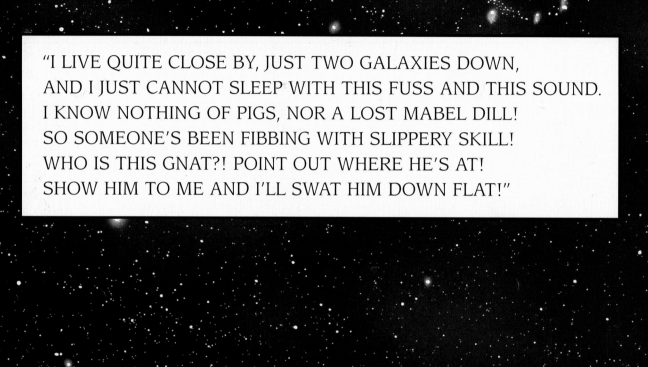

"I LIVE QUITE CLOSE BY, JUST TWO GALAXIES DOWN,
AND I JUST CANNOT SLEEP WITH THIS FUSS AND THIS SOUND.
I KNOW NOTHING OF PIGS, NOR A LOST MABEL DILL!
SO SOMEONE'S BEEN FIBBING WITH SLIPPERY SKILL!
WHO IS THIS GNAT?! POINT OUT WHERE HE'S AT!
SHOW HIM TO ME AND I'LL SWAT HIM DOWN FLAT!"

And that's what they did, each dad and each mother,
They pointed right up at my shaking big brother.

Edwurd dropped low; he was scared ten times double.
He'd fibbed *way* too big and was now in HUGE trouble!

Then wait...
    what's that sound?
       A voice small and fine.
    Everyone stopped. Whose was it?...

It was mine.

"Oh please," I called out. "It's my fault, don't you see?
I broke that blue pig! Edwurd's fib was for *me!*
So dear grumpy thing with three eyes in your head,
See that it's *me* you should swat down instead."
What could I do? Edwurd faced a big mess.
I told a fat fib . . . yes, I'd learned from the best.

I thought I'd be smooshed—smashed—
 SQUASHED right on down!
But that big face looked in with a *smile,*
 not a frown.
"I think," he said firmly,
 "you both are big fibsters.
But out where I live,
 we're not loved by our sisters.
Mine, by the way, I have left all alone.
And now I'll go back to her sleeping at home."
He looked at me odd,
 kind of sad, kind of blue.
"It sure would be nice to have one like you."

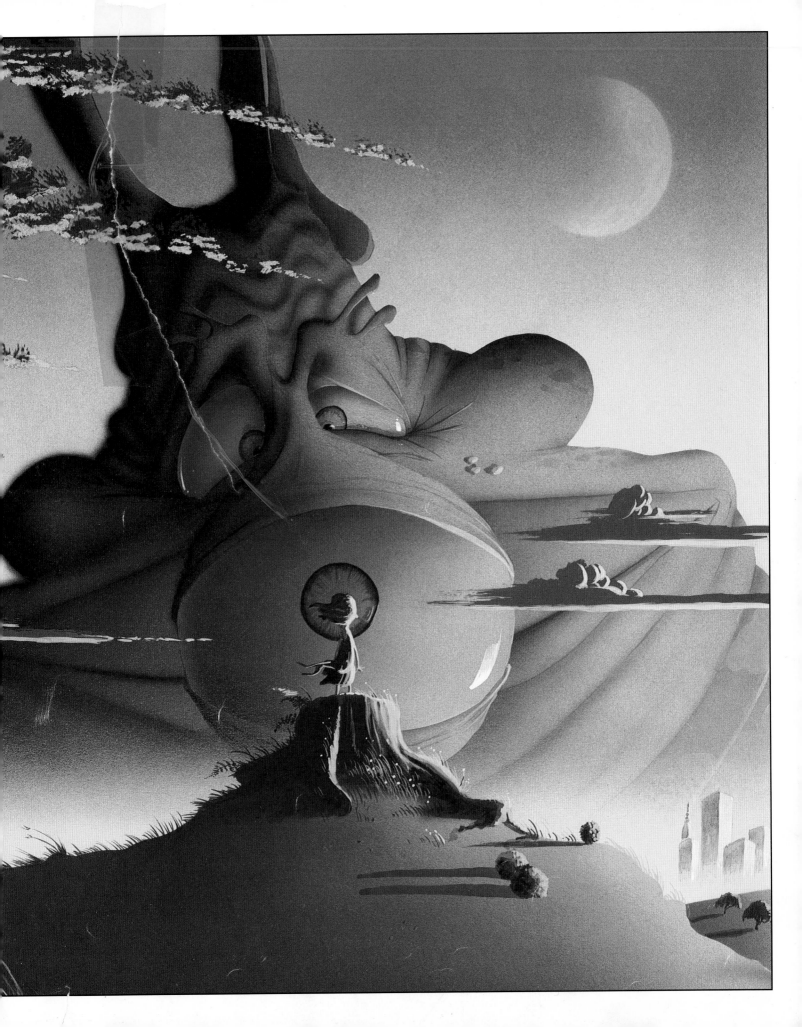

PUTT PUTT PUTT PUTT PUTT PUTT PUTT

Then he turned 'round his ship and back home he drove 'er,
And I turned to find Edwurd looking me over.
He said not a thing as we walked back to Dad,
Where there he looked up and confessed, "I've been bad."

So we taped and we glued and we fixed up Mom's pig,
And we told Mom the truth—that we'd fibbed—fat and big.

Our folks hugged us both, and collected no fines. . . .

...But we sat in Time Out to pay for our crimes.
Then Ed looked at me with a smile that was new
And said, "It *is* nice to have one like you."
Two former fibsters, that Edwurd and me,
But brother and sister we finally be.

And if somebody knows
Where Mabel Dill went,
Please tell her from Edwurd
That no harm was meant.